SHANNA'S Princess SHOW

by Jean Marzollo

Illustrated by **Shane W. Evans**

JUMP AT THE SUN
HYPERION BOOKS FOR CHILDREN
New York

I'm a royal princess.

Wonder how
I know?

I'll give you **5** clues
on today's Shanna Show.

Clue 1: tiara.
It sits beside my bed.

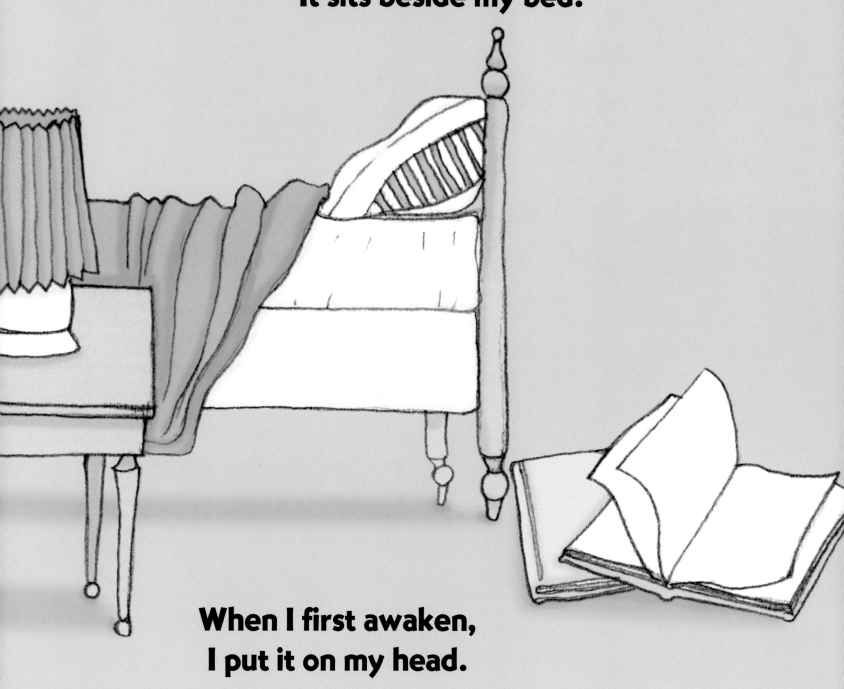

When I first awaken,
I put it on my head.

**Clue 2: every week
I have my friends for tea.**

**The ladies always curtsy,
and the gents all bow to me.**

And now we find we have arrived
at Clue Number 3.

Clue 4: sandwiches.
Dainty, small, and many.

**If you can't name the shape,
then you can't have any.**

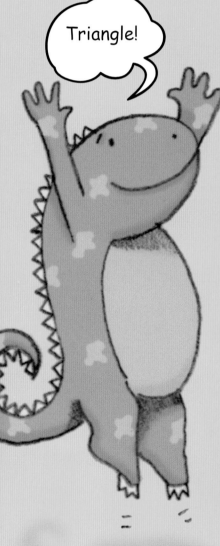

Triangle!

I want a square!

Grrrrr!
I wanted the
triangle!

**Now it's time for our review.
First me, then you.**